Robie H. Harris

I AM NOT GOING TO SCHOOL TODAY!

illustrated by Jan Ormerod

MARGARET K. McELDERRY BOOKS
NEW YORK LONDON TORONTO SYDNEY SINGAPORE

THANK YOU!

THANKS TO ALL OF YOU FOR SHARING YOUR EXPERTISE ABOUT YOUNG CHILDREN:

SARAH BIRSS, M.D., child analyst and pediatrician, Cambridge, MA

DEBORAH CHAMBERLAIN, research associate, Norwood, MA

BEN HARRIS, elementary school teacher, New York, NY

BILL HARRIS, parent, Cambridge, MA

DAVID HARRIS, prekindergarten/kindergarten teacher, New York, NY

ROBYN HEILBRUN, parent, Salt Lake City, UT

ELLEN KELLEY, director, The Cambridge-Ellis School, Cambridge, MA

ELIZABETH A. LEVY, children's book author, New York, NY

JANET PATTERSON, prekindergarten teacher, Shady Hill School, Cambridge, MA

KAREN SHORR, prekindergarten teacher, The Brookwood School, Manchester, MA

Margaret K. McElderry Books
An imprint of Simon & Schuster Children's Publishing Division
1230 Avenue of the Americas, New York, New York 10020
Text copyright © 2003 by Bee Productions, Inc.
Illustration copyright © 2003 by Jan Ormerod
All rights reserved including the right of reproduction in whole or in part in any form.
Book design by Abelardo Martínez
The text for this book is set in Sabon.
The illustrations are rendered in black pencil line and watercolor washes.
Manufactured in China
8 10 9 7
Library of Congress Cataloging-in-Publication Data
Harris, Robie H.
I am NOT going to school today / by Robie Harris ; illustrated by Jan Ormerod.
p. cm.
Summary: A little boy decides to skip his very first day of school, because on the first day
one doesn't know anything, but on the second, one knows everything.
ISBN-13: 978-0-689-83913-9 ISBN-10: 0-689-83913-8
[1. First day of school—Fiction. 2. Schools—Fiction.] I. Ormerod, Jan, ill. II. Title.
PZ7.H2436 Iab 2001
[E]—dc21
00-048053

For Ben—because it's your story!
—R. H. H.

For Paul Bryant
—J. O.

The night before the very first day of school, I put a banana, a shiny silver flashlight, a wind-up chicken, a pair of mittens, and a tiny box of raisins into my backpack. Then I put my new backpack at the end of my bed—right next to Hank.

I put my underpants, socks, shorts, a dinosaur T-shirt, and my new sneakers with the green stripes at the end of my bed too. I was ready for the very first day of school.

Daddy came in to read me a story. And Mommy came to tuck me in tight. They both gave me a hug and a kiss good night. Just before they turned out the light, I put Hank right next to me. Because Hank's my friend.

I closed my eyes and held on tight to Hank. That's when I decided that going to the very first day of school was NOT a good idea.

The very next morning, as soon as I woke up, I ran to Mommy and Daddy's room. I stood right next to their bed and shouted, "I am NOT going to school today!"

"Why?" asked Mommy as she sat up and put on her glasses.

"Why not?" asked Daddy as he sat up and stretched his arms.

"Because on the very first day of school, you don't know anything!" I told them.

"You don't know all the kids' names,

  or which cubby is your cubby,

  or where the crayons are,

  or what kind of juice they have,

  or if they have crackers—at all!"

Then I jumped onto their bed and said,
"And on the very first day of school,
    you don't know any of the songs,
    or when it's story time,
    or where the toilet is,
    or if you can play in the rain.
    You don't know anything—at all!
    That's why I am NOT going to school today.
    But I WILL go tomorrow—because on the
    second day of school, you know everything!"
    "But if you don't go today," said Daddy,
"what will you do all day?"
    "Hank and I will play all day," I said.
"That's what we like to do!"

"You know what? It's time to get up!" said Mommy.

"I'm already up," I said.

"Well, then it's time to get dressed!" said Daddy.

Daddy and Mommy got up. I went and got dressed. I brushed all my teeth. I pulled on my brand-new sneakers. I pulled the laces tight, but I couldn't tie them. I took Hank and went to eat my breakfast.

Daddy tied my laces with double knots. And he made blueberry pancakes—my favorite. I ate every bite and I drank all my milk.

Then Daddy looked at his watch and said, "It's time to go to school."

"I told you!" I said as I held on tight to Hank and slid under the table. "I am NOT going to school today!"

Daddy bent down and gave me a kiss.

"I can't go!" I cried. "Hank will miss me! And I'll miss Hank!"

"Hank will miss you," Mommy called from the front hall. "But I think he will be fine."

"No, he won't!" I said as I crawled out from under the table. "I can't leave Hank. And if I go to school, Hank won't have anyone to play with."

I carried Hank to the front hall. "Hank does NOT want me to go to school today!" I said. "Hank needs me here!"

"I have an idea," said Mommy. "You could take Hank to school today."

"But if Hank comes to school," I said, "Hank won't know anything!"

"Hank will know you," said Mommy. "And Hank won't have to stay home."

I looked at Hank and said, "Hank, you won't be lonely if you go to school with me."

Daddy looked at me and said, "It's almost time to leave!"

"And Hank, you won't miss the first day of school," I said, "if you go with me."

"Then we'd better get going!" said Mommy.

I ran to my room and grabbed my backpack. I put Hank in. I made sure his head was sticking out the top—so he could see. I slipped my backpack on my back. I put two pennies in my pocket for good luck—one for Hank and one for me. Then it was time to go. And Hank went with me.

At school, the teacher said how happy he was to meet me.
He told me his name was Mr. Chase.
I showed him Hank.
He showed me my cubby.

Then we all sat in a circle and we told everyone our names.
The other teacher told us her name too.
Her name was Ms. Chen.

Mr. Chase showed us where the crayons were.
He showed us where the toilets were.

And then it was time for juice—orange juice.
And we all got to eat crackers with yellow cheese.

Mr. Chase told us that when it rains a little,
we can still go out to play.

But if rains a whole lot, we'll play inside.

We sang a song about a train that was down by the station.
And I knew all the words. Mr. Chase said we would sing
lots of songs—every day.

Then it was story time. Ms. Chen said
we would have story time—every day.

After that, it was time to go home.
So Mr. Chase said, "See you tomorrow!"

That night I packed my backpack and put it at the end of my bed. I got into bed and put Hank right next to me. Then I told Mommy and Daddy, "Hank liked going to school today. And I think he'll go to school tomorrow—if I come with him."

Mommy and Daddy gave me a hug and a kiss good night and turned out the light. I held on tight to Hank.

Then I whispered, "Hank, I liked going to school today.
I bet you did too.
And I WILL go to school tomorrow—
if you come with me."

And he did.